VROOM, VROOM!

Poems About Things with Wheels

Lee Aucoin, *Creative Director*
Jamey Acosta, *Senior Editor*
Heidi Fiedler, *Editor*
Produced and designed by
Denise Ryan & Associates
Illustration © Paul Nicholls
Rachelle Cracchiolo, *Publisher*

Teacher Created Materials
5301 Oceanus Drive
Huntington Beach, CA 92649-1030
http://www.tcmpub.com
Paperback: ISBN: 978-1-4333-5521-9
Library Binding: ISBN: 978-1-4807-1689-6
© 2014 Teacher Created Materials

Selected by
Mark Carthew

Illustrated by
Paul Nicholls

Contents

Fire Engine 4

What a Load! 6

Song of the Train 8

The Robot 12

The Yellow Bus 14

The Wondrous Crane 16

Engineers 18

Vroom, Vroom 20

Tractors, Trucks, Trains,
and Trams 22

Sources and
Acknowledgements 24

Fire Engine

"Come and see the flashing light
On the fire engine bright!
See it racing down the road
Carrying its heavy load!"
So said Thomasina Brown
Just before it ran her down.

Doug MacLeod

What a Load!

A monster that traveled by rail
Turned porters and
train drivers pale.
He had to be stuck
on a very large truck
While another one
carried his tail.

Max Fatchen

Song of the Train

Clickety-clack,
Wheels on the track,
This is the way
They begin the attack:
Click-ety-clack,
Click-ety-clack,
Click-ety, clack-ety,
Click-ety
Clack.

Clickety-clack,
Over the crack,
Faster and faster
The song of the track:
Clickety-clack,
Clickety-clack,
Clickety, clackety,
Clackety,
Clack.

Riding in front,
Riding in back,
Everyone hears
The song of the track:
Clickety-clack,
Clickety-clack,
Clickety, clickety,
Clackety,
Clack.

David McCord

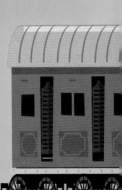

The Robot

My switch clicks on,
My eyes light up,
My motor starts the rumbles.
My cogs and gears all creak
    and crank.
My radar turns and tumbles.
My program data bank
    boots up,
It tells me what to do...
I'm WL-3-61.
Now, how can I help you?

Mark Carthew

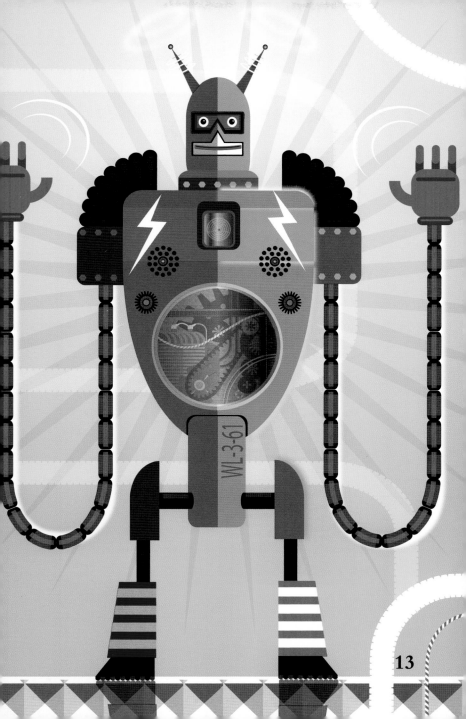

The Yellow Bus

Step aboard the yellow bus
  and bump along the road
  with us.
Every day, at every stop, the
  bus pulls up and on we hop.
Along the same route every
  day, it motors on its
  merry way.
Here it comes along our street,
  full of laughter, friends,
  and feet.

Mark Carthew

The Wondrous Crane

No need to explain
the wondrous crane;
    it lifts and lowers
    fast and slowers
    stops and goers
    again and again!

Janeen Brian

Engineers

Pistons, valves, and wheels
   and gears—
      That's the life of engineers.
      Thumping, chunking engines
      going,
      Hissing steam and whistles
      blowing.
There's not a place I'd rather be
      Than working 'round
      machinery,
      Listening to that clanking
      sound,
      Watching all the wheels go
      'round.

Jimmy Garthwaite

19

Vroom, Vroom

Where do the cars all come
   from,
Where do the cars all go?
Zooming down the highway
   to the city through the snow.
There are shiny shapes
   and colors,
Red, yellow, black, and blue.
Vroom! Vroom!
Engines roar
   through a street near you.

Mark Carthew

Tractors, Trucks, Trains, and Trams

Tractors,
Trucks,
Trains, and trams,
In the city,
Traffic jams!

Mark Carthew

23

Sources and Acknowledgements

Brian, Janeen. "The Wondrous Crane" from *Machino Supremo: Poems About Machines.* Victoria: Celapene Press, 2009. Reprinted by permission of Celapene Press, Knoxfield, Victoria.

Carthew, Mark. "The Robot" from *Machino Supremo: Poems About Machines.* Victoria: Celapene Press, 2009. Reprinted by permission of Celapene Press, Knoxfield, Victoria.

Carthew, Mark. "The Yellow Bus," "Tractors, Trucks, Trains, and Trams," and "Vroom, Vroom" were written especially for this anthology.

Fatchen, Max. "What a Load!" from *Meet the Monsters.* Australia: Scholastic, 2004. Reprinted by permission of Scholastic, Australia.

Garthwaite, Jimmy. "Engineers" from *Puddin' and Pie.* New York: Harper & Row, 1929, renewed 1957. Reprinted by permission of Harper & Row, New York.

MacLeod, Doug. "Fire Engine" from *In The Garden of Bad Things.* Australia: Penguin Books, 1981. Reprinted by permission of Penguin Books, Australia.

McCord, David. "Song of the Train" from *One at a Time.* New York: Hachette Book Group, Inc., 1952. Reprinted by permission of Hachette Book Group, Inc., New York.